BEBOP EXPRESS

Special Thanks to
Twin City Model Railroad Museum, Minnesota Transportation Museum,
Via's Vintage Wear, and Joe, Ron, Ethel, Michael, Vincent, and Josie.

Bebop Express

Library of Congress Cataloging-in-Publication Data
Panahi, H. L. (Heather L.)
Bebop Express / by H. L. Panahi ; illustrated by Steve Johnson and Lou Fancher. —
1st ed.
   p.   cm.
   Summary: A rollicking rhythmic express train takes passengers on a jazzy
journey that celebrates the United States and its unique musical culture.
   ISBN 0-06-057190-X — ISBN 0-06-057191-8 (lib. bdg.)
   [1. Railroads—Trains—Fiction. 2. Jazz—Fiction. 3. Stories in rhyme.]
I. Johnson, Steve, date, ill.   II. Fancher, Lou, ill.   III. Title.
PZ8.3.P1573Be 2005
[E]—dc22
                                                          2003024244
                                                                CIP
                                                                AC

Book Design by Lou Fancher
1 2 3 4 5 6 7 8 9 10
❖
First Edition

To Shahriar, Nora, and Maya—
You make my life a groovin' and movin',
nonstoppin' boppin' adventure.
—H.L.P.

To our family and friends,
who bebop on these pages.
—S.J. & L.F.

BebOP ExPReSS

by **H. L. Panahi**

illustrated by **Steve Johnson** and **Lou Fancher**

LAURA GERINGER BOOKS
An Imprint of HarperCollins Publishers

Amistad

The whistle's a-blowin', the engine's a-pumpin'—
conductors are dancin' and passengers jumpin'!
Quick! Climb aboard the Bebop Express.
It's the jazziest train from the east to the west.
Chug-a chug-a chug-a chug-a Choo! Choo!
Chug-a chug-a chug-a chug-a Choo! Choo!

Last stop! New Orleans—for a musical treat,
a traffic-jam jammin' show out in the street.
People will come from all over the place
to see Sax Man get down with the smooth groovin' bass.
Song Lady will scat to the **beboppin' sound,**
while Drum Man shuffles and scuffles around.

They'll be skippin' it, rippin' it,
hummin' and drummin' it,
slappin' it, tappin' it,
finger-and-**thumbin'** it,
flailin' and wailin' it,
swingin' and swayin' it.
People will clap along
while they are **playin'** it.

European Arrival

European explorers of the 1600s described the Lenni Lenape as peaceful, friendly people. But as more settlers came and took their land, the Lenni Lenape grew unfriendly. Often, they were forced to sign **treaties** they didn't understand. Other times, settlers simply moved onto Lenni Lenape land.

In addition to losing land, many Lenni Lenape died from European diseases. By 1700, nearly all of them were gone from New Jersey. They had either died from illness or been forced to move away.

▲ In the early 1600s, European explorers traded with the Lenni Lenape.

FACT!

Many Lenni Lenape live in Oklahoma and Canada today.

7

Chapter 2

Early Settlers

The first Europeans to settle in what became New Jersey were Dutch traders. They began the New Amsterdam Colony in 1623. New Amsterdam covered parts of present-day New York and New Jersey. The Dutch traded with American Indians for animal furs. At that time, fur coats and hats were stylish in Europe.

In 1638, Swedish settlers came to North America to build a fur-trading colony. They named the colony New Sweden. It covered parts of what is now New Jersey and Delaware. The Swedish and Dutch colonies fought over land. In 1655, the Dutch took over New Sweden.

Colonial borders were set in 1763. New Jersey's borders were set by water in all directions but north. ➡

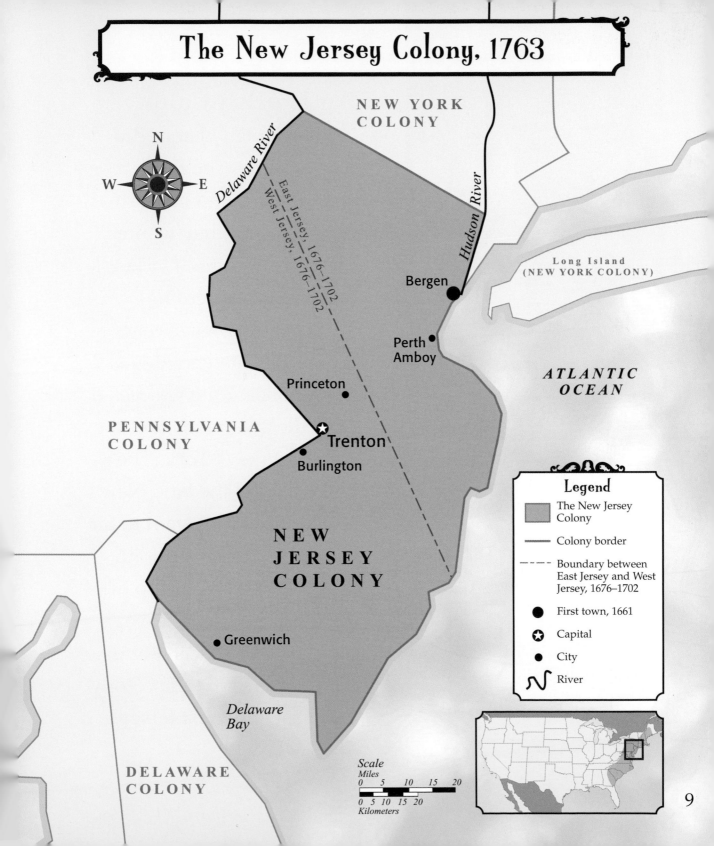

The New Jersey Colony, 1763

NEW YORK COLONY

Delaware River

East Jersey, 1676–1702

West Jersey, 1676–1702

Hudson River

Bergen

Perth Amboy

Long Island (NEW YORK COLONY)

ATLANTIC OCEAN

Princeton

PENNSYLVANIA COLONY

Trenton

Burlington

NEW JERSEY COLONY

Greenwich

Delaware Bay

DELAWARE COLONY

Legend

The New Jersey Colony

Colony border

Boundary between East Jersey and West Jersey, 1676–1702

First town, 1661

Capital

City

River

Scale
Miles
0 5 10 15 20
0 5 10 15 20
Kilometers

9

↟ The Duke of York gave New Jersey its name before he gave the land away.

FACT!

Sir George Carteret once governed the Island of Jersey, near England. The name New Jersey honored his service.

An English Colony

The Dutch victory did not last long. The English already had land in North America, and they wanted more. In 1664, England took over New Amsterdam.

In the following years, the colony changed owners many times. King Charles II gave the area to his brother James, Duke of York. The Duke named the land New Jersey. He then gave it to Sir George Carteret and John Lord Berkeley. A group of **Quakers** bought Berkeley's half. In 1676, Carteret and the Quakers split the colony into East and West Jersey.

Many Faiths

Unlike other colonies, New Jersey allowed freedom of religion. People of many faiths came there. Baptists and other **protestants** settled in East Jersey. They built towns and villages. Quakers remained in West Jersey. It became an area of large farms.

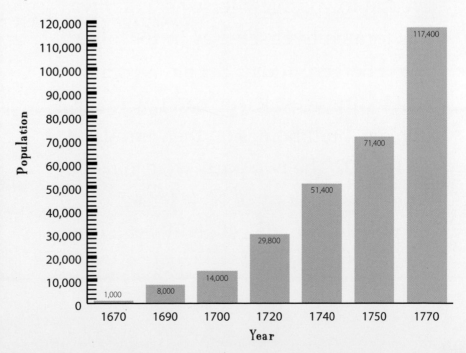

Population Growth of the New Jersey Colony

11

Chapter 3

Colonial Life

The first New Jersey settlers built log homes. They filled spaces between the logs with mud or grass. Thin wooden shingles covered the roofs. Oiled paper covered window openings.

The two parts of New Jersey were set up differently. In East Jersey, settlers lived in towns. New Jersey's first town was formed in East Jersey in 1661. It was called Bergen. Today, Bergen is part of Jersey City. West Jersey had few towns. Quakers built homes on their farmland.

In 1702, the two parts were joined as the royal colony of New Jersey. But the ways of life in East and West Jersey remained different.

In West Jersey, Quakers lived on large farms spread out from each other.

Life on the Farm

New Jersey's first colonists farmed to survive. They grew oats, wheat, and corn. Farmers also raised cows, sheep, and chickens. These animals provided milk, wool, meat, and eggs.

Colonists also made their own clothes. Men used deerskin to make leather coats and pants. Women made cloth from wool or plants.

Colonial women used spinning wheels to make yarn. ▼

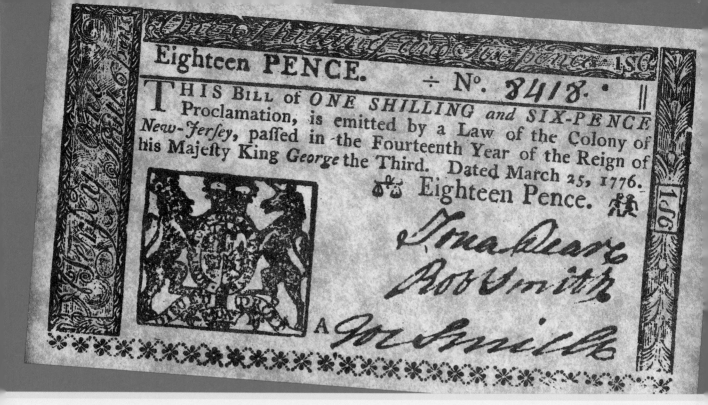

Eighteen **PENCE.** ÷ Nº. *8418.*

THIS BILL of **ONE SHILLING** and SIX-PENCE Proclamation, is emitted by a Law of the Colony of *New-Jersey*, passed in the Fourteenth Year of the Reign of his Majesty King *George* the Third. Dated March 25, 1776. Eighteen Pence.

▲ The New Jersey Colony printed its own money.

Struggles over land were common in early New Jersey. Some people paid the Dutch or Swedish government for their land. Others bought land from American Indians. When England took over, the government expected these settlers to pay them too. Many colonists refused to pay the English. At times, colonists fought the government over land.

Chapter 4

Work and Trade

At first, farming was the most common work in New Jersey. But as towns grew, jobs changed. People didn't have to farm to survive anymore. Towns needed millers, blacksmiths, and wheel makers.

New Jersey's First Factories

Some colonists opened factories. In 1642, Aert T. van Putten built America's first brewery in Hoboken. Ironworks opened near Shrewsbury around 1670.

In 1760, the Campbell family started an unusual business in Bergen. They built a wampum factory.

Speedwell Ironworks was located in Morristown, New Jersey.

American Indians and settlers used wampum belts as money. Indians made wampum beads from seashells and strung them into belts. The Campbells made wampum beads by machine.

New Jersey Farmers

Many people still farmed in New Jersey, especially in the southern part. Farmers grew rice, corn, and other grains. They raised cattle and horses. Some farmers had orchards filled with apple, pear, plum, and cherry trees. They sold their goods to traders. Traders sold goods to people in other colonies, England, and the Carribean Islands.

New Jersey farmers tended to many crops and animals. ▼

Finding Workers

Farms and factories both needed workers. At first, **indentured servants** served as workers. They were poor immigrants who could not afford the trip to America. Local settlers paid for them to come to America. The settler owned the servant for a fixed number of years. The servant was free to go, after he or she had worked off the debt.

By 1700, slaves took the place of indentured servants. Ships brought slaves from Africa to New Jersey. Slaves worked their entire lives without pay.

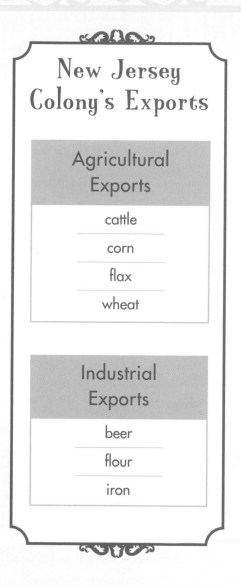

New Jersey Colony's Exports

Agricultural Exports
cattle
corn
flax
wheat

Industrial Exports
beer
flour
iron

The first Baptist church in West Jersey was built in 1690 in Salem County. Baptists had split off from the Church of England. They believed people shouldn't be baptized until they were adults.

Presbyterians lived in New Jersey's Cohansey River Valley. William Tennent and his four sons were ministers there. In the 1730s, they traveled the colonies, preaching about Christianity with great excitement. Other ministers began to follow their lead. Their sermons moved many people. A renewed Christian spirit swept through the colonies. This period is called the Great Awakening.

◀ The sermons during the Great Awakening moved many people to tears.

FACT!

In 1726, William Tennent founded the Log College to train ministers. Today, the Log College is Princeton University.

Chapter 6

Becoming a State

By the 1760s, American colonists had developed their own way of life. Some people thought the colonies were outgrowing Great Britain's rule. This idea spread when Britain began to tax paper, tea, and sugar.

The taxes upset many American colonists. They had no **representatives** in Britain's government. Because of this, colonists believed Britain had no right to tax them. In 1774, colonists in Greenwich, New Jersey, protested the taxes. They burned a shipload of British tea.

The Proclamation of 1763 set colonial borders. The Atlantic Ocean was New Jersey's eastern border. ➤

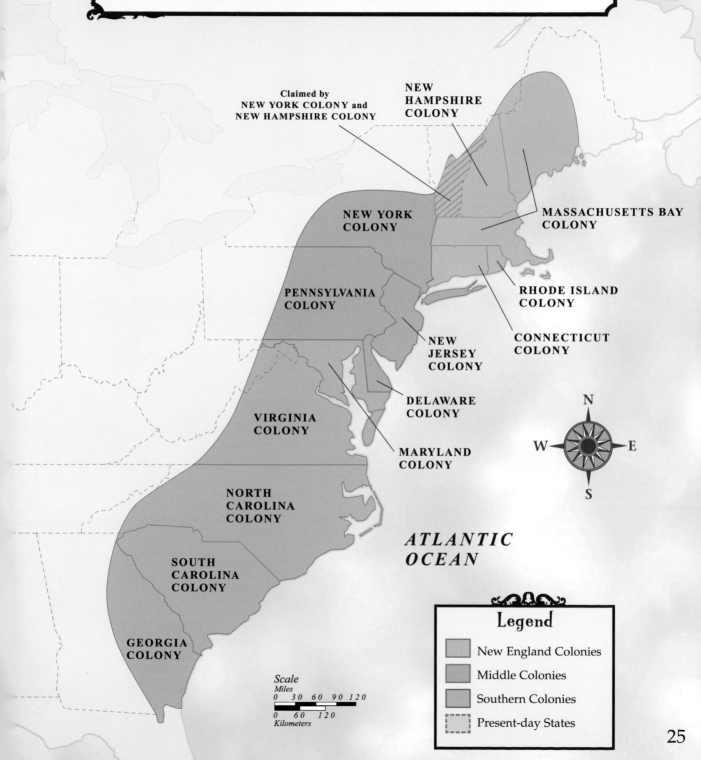

The Thirteen Colonies, 1763

Claimed by
NEW YORK COLONY and
NEW HAMPSHIRE COLONY

NEW
HAMPSHIRE
COLONY

NEW YORK
COLONY

MASSACHUSETTS BAY
COLONY

PENNSYLVANIA
COLONY

RHODE ISLAND
COLONY

CONNECTICUT
COLONY

NEW
JERSEY
COLONY

DELAWARE
COLONY

VIRGINIA
COLONY

MARYLAND
COLONY

NORTH
CAROLINA
COLONY

ATLANTIC
OCEAN

SOUTH
CAROLINA
COLONY

N
W   E
S

GEORGIA
COLONY

Scale
Miles
0   30 60 90 120

0   60   120
Kilometers

Legend
New England Colonies
Middle Colonies
Southern Colonies
Present-day States

25

Birth of a Nation

In 1774, each colony sent representatives to the Continental Congress. This group tried to reason with Great Britain. But in 1775, the Revolutionary War began.

On July 2, 1776, New Jersey approved its first state **constitution**. Congress declared the United States' **independence** from Great Britain two days later.

During the Revolutionary War, nearly 100 battles were fought in New Jersey. The British wanted to control New Jersey. Their goal was to divide the northern and southern colonies.

The Battle of Trenton was the most important New Jersey battle. On the night of December 25, 1776, George Washington quietly led his troops across the Delaware River. They made a surprise attack. Washington and his men won the battle.

America won the war in 1783. The nation's leaders wrote the United States Constitution in 1787. This document set up the U.S. government. New Jersey approved the Constitution on December 18, 1787 and became the third state.

◀ George Washington's victory in the Battle of Trenton raised the spirits of many Americans. They had been losing the war up to that point.

27

Fast Facts

Name
The New Jersey Colony (named for the Island of Jersey, England)

Location
Middle colonies

Year of Founding
1623

First Settlement
New Amsterdam Colony

Colony's Founders
Dutch traders

Religious Faiths
Baptist, Presbyterian, Puritan, Quaker

Agricultural Products
Cattle, corn, flax, wheat

Major Industry
Ironworks

Population in 1770
117,400 people

Statehood
December 18, 1787 (3rd state)

Time Line

1676
Sir George Carteret and a group of Quakers divide colony into East and West Jersey.

1664
England takes over New Amsterdam.

1655
The Dutch take over New Sweden. It becomes part of New Amsterdam.

1638
Swedish traders set up the New Sweden Colony.

1707
An Act of Union unites England, Wales, and Scotland; they become the United Kingdom of Great Britain.

1763
Proclamation of 1763 sets colonial borders and provides land for American Indians.

1623
Dutch traders set up the New Amsterdam Colony.

1775
American colonies begin fight for their independence from Great Britain in the Revolutionary War.

1776
Declaration of Independence is approved in July.

1783
America wins the Revolutionary War.

1787
On December 18, New Jersey is the third state to join the United States.

Glossary

constitution (kon-stuh-TOO-shuhn)—the written system of laws in a state or country that state the rights of the people and the powers of the government

indentured servant (in-DEN-churd SUR-vuhnt)—someone who agrees to work for another person for a certain length of time in exchange for travel expenses, food, and housing

independence (in-di-PEN-duhnss)—being free from the control of other people

protestant (PROT-uh-stuhnt)—describes Christians who do not belong to the Roman Catholic or the Orthodox church

Quaker (KWAY-kur)—a member of the Religious Society of Friends, a religious group founded in the 1600s, that prefers simple religious services and opposes war

representative (rep-ri-ZEN-tuh-tiv)—someone who is chosen to speak or act for others

treaties (TREE-tees)—official agreements between two or more groups or countries

Internet Sites

FactHound offers a safe, fun way to find Internet sites related to this book. All of the sites on FactHound have been researched by our staff.

Here's how:

1. Visit *www.facthound.com*
2. Type in this special code **0736826785** for age-appropriate sites. Or enter a search word related to this book for a more general search.
3. Click on the **Fetch It** button.

FactHound will fetch the best sites for you!

Read More

Italia, Bob. *The New Jersey Colony*. The Colonies. Edina, Minn.: Abdo, 2001.

Nobleman, Marc Tyler. *The Thirteen Colonies*. We the People. Minneapolis: Compass Point Books, 2002.

Weatherly, Myra. *The New Jersey Colony*. Our Thirteen Colonies. Chanhassen, Minn.: Child's World, 2004.

Index